THE DONNER PARTY

A DIARY OF A SURVIVOR

HISTORICAL FICTION BY
TOD OLSON

SCHOLASTIC INC.

New York   Toronto   London   Auckland   Sydney
Mexico City   New Delhi   Hong Kong

ILLUSTRATIONS BY
MATT COLLINS

ISBN 0-439-05700-0

SCHOLASTIC, READ 180, and associated logos and designs are
trademarks and/or registered trademarks of Scholastic Inc.
LEXILE is a trademark of MetaMetrics, Inc.

16 15   23   10 09 08

Virginia Reed dreamed of going West. But her trip became a gruesome nightmare.

INTRODUCTION

Virginia Reed was 12 years old in 1846. She and her family were headed for California in a group of covered wagons.

They had crossed 1,000 miles of dry plains, hot deserts, and high mountains. They still had 900 to go. And time was running out.

In November, howling snowstorms would hit the last mountains on the trail. The path would be buried under tons of snow.

If they didn't make it by then, they would be trapped. They would have to camp in the freezing snow and wait.

They might still make it to California. Or they might starve to death first.

Thousands of people went West in the 1840s. They all had dreams like Virginia's.

They hoped to find land with good soil. They longed for warm, sunny weather. Most of them made it.

Virginia's group was not so lucky. Eighty-eight of them reached the mountains. Nearly half of them died there.

In the mountains, the survivors faced a gruesome choice. They were running out of food. All they had left were the dead bodies of their friends and family. How far would they go to stay alive?

The group is now known as the Donner Party. It was named after two brothers who organized the journey.

A girl named Virginia Reed really did travel with the Donner Party. This diary is fiction. But it is based on that awful year in Virginia's life.

We're close to California. We decide to take a shortcut. But it isn't short at all.

SHORTCUT 1

July 31, 1846. We left Fort Bridger today. Papa, Mama, little Patty, and I are traveling with 23 other wagons. I ride Billy, my pony. Cash the dog walks alongside.

We have three wagons for all our things. Twenty oxen pull them. Papa and Milt Elliott and Baylis Williams drive our oxen.

The men are arguing. One says we will be buried in snow before we reach California.

I'm sure he's just nervous. It is so hot that I had to find an oak tree for shade. And besides, Papa says he knows of a shortcut.

I cannot wait till we get to California. My friend John says he will find gold. He'll share it with me. And we'll live like kings.

August 3. We met riders coming east. They warned us not to take the shortcut. But Papa says he read that the trail is good.

Four oxen are dead from drinking poisoned water. Their bellies were full like balloons.

August 12. I cannot ride Billy anymore. The brush is too thick now. There is no trail. We must make our own trail as we go.

The men cut down trees and bushes. They move huge rocks out of the way.

And we go . . . one . . . two miles every day. Time is as slow as a wagon wheel. I count the spokes . . . one . . . two . . . three.

August 20. We have spent three weeks on the shortcut. Papa said it would take only one. The men say that Papa chose the wrong route. One man said Papa will be a murderer if anyone dies. But John says that everyone must take care of themselves on the trail.

The desert steals everything we own. And it nearly takes our lives.

DESERT DAYS 2

September 1, 1846. The forest has let us go. Now the desert waits to swallow us. We are resting near a big salty lake. The men are packing grass into the wagons. We don't want the cattle to starve.

September 5. We've spent two days in the desert. Still we cannot see the end. The day is as hot as a frying pan. At night we freeze.

I cannot speak well. My tongue is big and dry, like a rag in my mouth.

Patty was crying for water. Papa yelled at her. Then he was ashamed of himself.

The oxen ran away to find water. Now there are none left to pull the wagons. So we left the wagons behind for now.

Billy has dropped to the ground. His tongue hangs into the sand.

September 6. We've walked all night. I'm lying with Mama and Patty. The dogs are our blankets. It's so cold. I'm too weak to write.

September 8. We are resting at a water hole. We only found six of our oxen here. So we went back and got just one wagon. We are leaving most of our things behind.

Mama kept her shawl and left her mirror. I kept my diary and left my summer hat. I kept my Bible and left my leather shoes. Papa says we will come back and get everything. But I never want to see this place again.

We left Billy lying stiff in the sand.

Virginia has lost almost everything that's important to her. What might she be thinking about this trip?

Papa is thrown out of the group. And our hope goes with him.

MURDER! 3

September 13, 1846. We are finally out of the desert.

There is not much food left. We sit down to watery soup at breakfast. We eat dried beef and biscuits at night.

Papa went hunting yesterday. He caught only a skinny rabbit. I know he is worried. Still, he tries to cheer us. He says we will soon eat fresh fruit and meat in California.

A storm came last night and painted the hilltops white with snow.

October 5. I thought we had seen trouble in the desert! But we didn't know. . . .

I must be calm and tell what happened. A driver named John Snyder was pushing his team up a steep hill. He was beating his cattle with a whip.

Papa saw him do it. He told Snyder to stop. "The animals are our only hope," he said. "And we have so few left." They argued. Then Snyder hit Papa with his whip handle. Blood began to run.

Mama stepped in. John Snyder hit her, too. Quickly, Papa pulled out his hunting knife. Snyder fell to the ground. He is dead. Now some of the men want Papa to be hanged!

October 6. Papa has been thrown out.

He had only a bony horse to ride. I could not let him go like that. After dark, John and I rode after him. I gave him some dried meat. I threw my arms around him. He said he would make it to California. Then he would bring us food. But I don't know. . . .

We try to get to California before winter. Then fear
makes us all act like animals.

RACING THE SNOW

October 8, 1846. Our oxen groan with effort. Their ribs push against their skin. My dog Cash barks and bites at their ankles. But they move like snails.

Each day we pass things left behind on the trail. Today I saw a desk, then a family's Sunday clothes, then a chest of toys. The trail is stripping us to the bone.

Sometimes I just want to lie down on the trail. I don't care if I ever get to California.

October 9. An old man named Hardkoop couldn't keep up. No one would let him ride. So he dropped behind. We think he is dead.

I pray for Papa at night.

October 12. The ground is wet and muddy. It smells of dead things. Beyond this marsh, there's another desert. Beyond that, there are the Sierra Nevada mountains. Beyond the mountains is California. We are in a race with snow and hunger.

John's pony fell into a bog. No one would help us pull it out. It twisted and splashed. Then it disappeared.

October 18. Every day we get closer to the mountaintops. On the other side is California. I would give anything to get there.

Snow fell again, ahead of us. White spreads down the mountain toward us.

Virginia says that they are "in a race with snow and hunger." What does she mean?

We've come so close . . . but our dreams are sunk in an ocean of snow.

TRAPPED! 5

October 28. Now, snow is everywhere. First it came in tiny, wet flakes. I thought of Christmas. Now it falls like knives. Every flake stings my face. We are so close to the pass. But we move so slowly.

October 31. We are buried in white. I sink to my waist. Every step drains my strength. I wait. Then I take another step. All day I hear the cries of mothers, babies, and men.

November 1. We have set fire to a tall pine. I am writing by its light. I pray no more snow comes tonight.

November 2. When I slept last night, John

stood under a tree. He was wrapped in a blanket. When I awoke he was still there. He was covered in white. All night he stood, just watching.

This morning it was decided. We cannot reach the pass. We must build shelters. We must try to find food. We will be here until the snow melts.

I pray that we can last that long.

Do you think that the group has made a wise decision? Or is this the beginning of the end?

We make a home in the mountains. And we try to hang on.

SNOWED IN 6

November 11, 1846. For a week, it has snowed. We have built four huts. They are made of crooked logs. We made the roofs from blankets and animal hides. There is a fireplace of rocks inside. Sixty people are here. The Donners and some others are nearby.

Mama bought two cattle from a man named Mr. Graves. She promised to pay him when we get to California. We killed the cattle and buried the meat in the snow.

November 27. White. It's the color of clean sheets, clouds, potatoes, cream, the meat of a turkey. Now when the sun is out, everything is white. White burns my eyes. If we can ever leave here, I never want to see white again.

December 12. Every day it snows. Sometimes we cannot go out for days. We shovel snow from the fireplace each morning. We chip wood from the sides of the cabin. Then we burn it. My hands get warm if I almost touch the fire. But deep inside, I'm always cold. I shake so much. I hope someone will be able to read this.

December 13. Baylis Williams is ill. He drove our oxen 1,800 miles. But it is 100 more miles to California. John tried to give him food today. He cannot eat.

December 15. Baylis Williams is dead. We buried him in a mound of snow. I once thought heaven was all white. Now I'm sure it's not.

We run out of food. And we try to get over the mountains.

LIFE OR DEATH 7

December 30, 1846. A man named Charley died today. Someone grabbed his money, two watches, and jewelry. Another took his coat and clothes. They left his body in the snow.

January 2, 1847. Our beef is gone. We can't last much longer. Patty cries for food all morning. Then she's silent the rest of the day.

January 4. Our driver Milt, Mama, and I are leaving. Patty will die if we do not find some meat. I said good-bye to our dear Cash. John tried to give me some food. But I know he needs to eat, too. So I refused to take it.

January 5. Milt leads the way on

snowshoes. We follow. I try to walk on the snow's crust. But I fall through. A leg disappears. I pull it out. I keep crawling.

January 6. My feet are very cold. They hurt so much. I have to crawl most of the day.

At night, Milt gets wood and builds a fire. He puts green logs on the bottom. That way the fire won't burn through the snow.

I found beef in my sack tonight. I am sure it's from John.

January 9. We were beaten by the mountain. We are back at the cabin.

Two nights ago, we awoke in a deep hole of snow. My feet were sitting in ice water. The fire had burned through the snow and we had fallen. When we woke up, we were ten feet down. We had to cut steps to get out.

Now I'm sitting at the fire. I'm warming my frozen feet. The pain comes like a hammer on my toes.

All our food is gone. We try to eat ox hides. Can it get any worse?

THE STARVING TIME 8

January 12, 1847. There's nothing left to eat. Mama took an ox hide from our roof. She boiled it on the fire. It turned into a thick paste. Mama spooned the mess onto our plates. I closed my eyes. I tried to imagine it was stew like we had at home. But I could not eat.

January 30. Mr. Graves took our hides yesterday. We bought cattle from him weeks ago. He took the hides as payment. His daughters are starving. We have only two hides left. And we have no roof at all. John's father has taken us in.

February 6. I cannot eat the hides. But there is nothing else. I fear I will die. We sit at night by the fire and pray. It is all we can do. Milt is even weaker than I.

February 8. Each night, John gives me half his food. It is a piece of beef as small as a coin. He looks at me. His mouth smiles. But his eyes do not.

February 9. Tonight we will eat Cash. John's father killed him with a knife. He is cooking him on the fire. The smell makes my mouth water. We will eat him in small pieces. He will feed us for three days.

What trouble we have seen. . . .

February 14. Milt is gone. We buried him in the snow. First we covered his feet and legs. Then we covered the rest of him. He is just a mound of snow. I hate to imagine what this awful place will be like when the snow melts.

February 15. Wolves dug up a body last

night. It wasn't Milt. The wolves dragged the body into the woods. Then they ate it. People here say we should do the same.

February 18. A man came from the Donners' camp. He said the people there are eating the dead. People here are talking about digging up Milt. But no one has moved to do it. I cannot do it myself. If someone else did it . . . I cannot say I would not eat.

People arrive from California to save us. And we fight the snow again.

RELIEF!

February 19, 1847. Yesterday evening, John heard a shout. He ran outside. Then he yelled back. "They're here! Thank God! They're here!" There are seven men from California. And there's some food.

February 21. Mama, Patty, and I are leaving. Only the strongest of us can go. There will be 23 of us.

John and his family are staying. It is terrible to see their faces. Other people will come to help. But I can't imagine staying here one more day. . . .

February 23. Will this mountain ever let us go? Patty cannot keep walking. Someone is taking her back to John's father. Mama wanted to go with her. But Patty said, "Please go find Papa."

We watched the men carry Patty away.

February 24. During the day, we walk. At night, we lie on the snow and sleep. When we awake, our clothes are frozen. We walk again. The sun melts the ice. Then our clothes are heavy, cold, and wet.

I am too weak to walk. I must crawl over each mound of snow. Mama stays ahead of me. She tells me we are getting closer to Papa. And she says there will soon be more food.

We are a family again—in California.

THE MIRACLE 10

February 27, 1847. Today I felt like giving up. Then we heard shouts from ahead. "Is Mrs. Reed with you? Tell her Mr. Reed is here!" Mama fell on the snow. I tried to run. I was gasping for air. Then I looked up. Papa was there. His pockets were full of bread.

February 28. Papa had to leave. He is going back to find Patty.

We have full bellies and a new spirit. Maybe now we can escape this white prison.

March 21. We are a family again. Papa is back. Patty is in bed. She can only drink soup and eat small bits of bread.

Papa had a horrible tale to tell. He

reached Patty in two days. He left with her and 15 others. But terrible snowstorms nearly buried them all alive. They had nothing to eat for four days.

Then three people died. The others knew they could die, too. They had no choice. They had to eat the dead to stay alive. For 11 days, they went on. Papa had to carry Patty. His feet bled in the snow.

Finally, we are all here in California.

April 8. I am sitting in a meadow. John is next to me. We're eating lamb, fresh-baked bread, and sweet grapes. Green is everywhere, green grass, green trees. I could sit here forever—in California.